Maisie Moe

NO BOYS ALLOWED!

Maise Mae Books

No Boys Allowed
Bad-Luck Bridesmaid
Camping is not very Ooh La La

Maisie Moe

NO BOYS ALLOWED!

Poppy Harper

Illustrated by Clare Elsom

LITTLE, BROWN BOOKS FOR YOUNG READERS
www.lbkids.co.uk

With special thanks to Dan Metcalf.

LITTLE, BROWN BOOKS FOR YOUNG READERS

First published in Great Britain in 2014 by Little, Brown Books for Young Readers
Reprinted 2014

A CIP catalogue record for this book
is available from the British Library.

ISBN 978-0-349-00153-1

Typeset in Humanist by M Rules
Printed and bound in Great Britain by
Clays Ltd, St Ives plc

Papers used by LBYR are from well-managed forests
and other responsible sources.

MIX
Paper from
responsible sources
FSC® C104740

Little, Brown Books for Young Readers
An imprint of
Little, Brown Book Group
100 Victoria Embankment
London EC4Y 0DY

An Hachette UK Company
www.hachette.co.uk

www.lbkids.co.uk

To Izalynn-next-door,
a super-fab friend

CHAPTER ONE

Worm-tastrophe

"Josh! Jack! I won't tell you again!" shrieked Mum, who was in the next room. "I don't care who started it! Get that dirty sock off your brother's head and get out of bed!"

Maisie Mae's eyes pinged open. It was Monday morning, which, like every morning in her house, was complete and utter **CHAOS**. In her shared bedroom, she pulled her duvet over her head and wished as hard as she could that something would happen to close school for the day, like a blizzard, or a flood, or an escaped herd of rampaging rhinoceroses. From under her covers, she could hear her other brothers, Harry and Ollie, the troublesome twins, whispering over on the other side of the room.

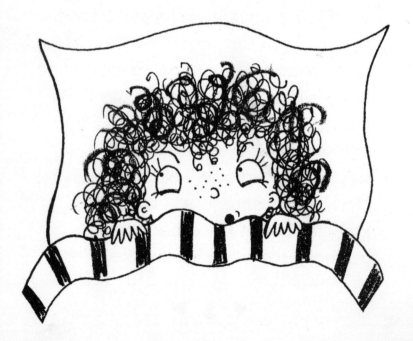

"I dare you to wear your pyjamas to school!"

"I will if you will …"

"Okay, **GO!**"

There was the sound of frantic messing about, followed by laughing and falling over. Maisie pulled the covers up higher.

"Right, up and at 'em, you lot!" yelled Mum as she flung open their bedroom door. "Come on, Maisie Mae, it's a brand new day!"

Maisie peeked out to see Mum standing in the doorway, still in her dressing gown. She had a cup of tea in one hand and held a snotty, grinning toddler balanced on her hip with the other. Arthur Stanley was Maisie's only younger brother. Maisie had wanted a baby sister so she could do nice

GIRLY things, like braid her hair and dress her up, but she quite liked Arthur Stanley, even though he was a boy. He hadn't learned to talk yet, so he never called her horrible names like her other brothers did. He smiled at her as he dribbled into Mum's cup of tea.

"Well done, boys!" Mum exclaimed. "I'm very impressed! Maisie Mae, perhaps you could follow the twins' example. They're already dressed."

Maisie looked over at the twins' side of the room. Harry and Ollie were standing in front of their bunk beds in their school uniforms, looking angelic.

Maisie sat up. "That doesn't count," she said. "Look, they've still got their pyjamas on under their school clothes."

"Quiet, bumface!" said Ollie.

"And they've got one of each other's shoes on!"

Sure enough, Harry was wearing two left shoes and Ollie was wearing two right ones.

"Hmm?" Mum said absently. "Oh, boys! Well, it'll have to do. Come and get breakfast, or you'll make your dad late for work."

Mum left, and the twins followed, jumping on Maisie Mae's bed on their way out.

"Nice try, bogey-breath!" said Harry. They ran out of the room and down the stairs, singing a song they'd made up:

"Maisie Mae, all brown
      and curly,

What a shame she's such a GIRLY!
Maisie Mae, she likes pink,
Looks like a pig and makes a STINK!"

Maisie **HATED** her brothers. She hated all *five* of them, but having to share a room with Harry and Ollie, the Gruesome Twosome, was the absolute **WORST**. The bedroom looked like someone had put a firecracker in a wardrobe full of clothes and let it explode all over the floor. The twins' bunk bed loomed over her like a tower of mess, and everything in the room screamed **BOY!** Her side of the room wasn't much better. Maisie sighed as she imagined the things a *proper* girl's room should have: a beautiful princess bed covered with heart-shaped cushions, a

huge toy-chest shaped
like a fairytale palace
and a framed picture of
a unicorn. Instead, she
had boring blue walls
and yucky grey carpet.

Her bed looked like a boy's, too. Her
duvet used to be her big brother Josh's,
and you could still see the picture of
Postman Pat on the faded fabric. Maisie
only had a few nice girly things, and she
had to keep them in a special box under
her bed marked HOMEWORK to stop her
horrible brothers from ruining them.

Maisie Mae got dressed quickly. If
you didn't get to breakfast fast enough in
her house, you wouldn't eat at all – her
brothers could scoff down a *whole* packet
of cereal in nine minutes and twenty-

seven seconds (she had timed them once). She grabbed her school bag and started pushing her books and pencil case inside. But her lunchbox wasn't there. Maisie was *sure* she hadn't taken it out of her bag.

Her lunchbox wasn't just any old lunchbox. It was an extra-special, perfectly pink Barbie lunchbox that Bethany-next-door had given to her for her birthday. She had *exactly* the same one so they could be just like twins – not horrible, snotty **BOY** twins like Harry and Ollie, but brilliant exactly-the-same-in-every-way **GIRL** twins.

Maisie wished that Bethany-next-door really *was* her twin, or even just her sister. Given the chance, Maisie Mae would swap any of her brothers for Bethany-next-door as a sister. Actually, she'd swap them *all*.

Maisie went to find Mum, who was in the bathroom with an electric toothbrush in her mouth and Arthur Stanley at her feet. The dribbling toddler was squeezing all the toothpaste out of its tube, making patterns on the floor with the red, white and blue stripes.

"Mum! Have you seen my extra-special, perfectly pink Barbie lunchbox?" Maisie asked.

"Gnooo," Mum burbled, spitting out a

mouthful of paste. "If you can't find it, use one of the boys' ones."

Maisie screwed her face up and glared at her mum fiercely. "*Mum!* I can't take a *boy's* lunchbox to school!"

Mum smiled and smoothed down a bit of Maisie's hair that was sticking out. "You might have to if you can't find yours. It's probably in your bombsite of a bedroom. Will you look again for me?"

Maisie Mae sighed and stomped off back to her room. "It's not just *my* room, is it?" she mumbled to herself. "It's Harry and Ollie's too. Which means it could be *anywhere*!"

She stood in the doorway and looked at the room. Somehow, it looked darker on the twins' side. Their army camouflage duvet covers and general chaos made it look like a scary forest, where a wild animal might jump on you at any second. Actually, a wild animal might explain the **DISGUSTING** snoring she heard at night from the bunk bed. Maisie took a deep breath and held her nose. She *had* to find that lunchbox.

She looked under duvets, in cupboards and even in the dirty-laundry bin (**GROSS!**), but she couldn't find it anywhere. She had her head in the twins' sock drawer when she heard a call.

"Maisie Mae! If you don't come down now, I'm going to feed your chocolatey chocolate-ball cereal to Arthur Stanley!" Dad yelled from downstairs.

"Coming!" called Maisie. Suddenly she saw her lunchbox, hidden behind a pair of old PE shorts under the bed. "AHA!" She grinned as she fished it out carefully, trying not to touch the shorts. Then she noticed how heavy it was. She lifted it up, knowing that whatever she was about to find wasn't going to be nice. She slowly opened the lid …

… to find a box full of pink, squiggling, squirming, wormy **WORMS!**

"Aaaaagghh!" screamed Maisie Mae. "I HATE boys!"

AAAARGGHH!

CHAPTER TWO

Sandwich Surprise

At school, Maisie Mae sat in the lunch hall with Bethany-next-door, their matching lunchboxes side by side. Bethany looked perfect as usual, with a clean, ironed dress, shiny, pink glasses and a pink hairclip in her long, straight blonde hair. Maisie Mae was wearing a holey hand-me-down school jumper and her crazy, curly hair was sticking up everywhere – Maisie had put a hairslide

in it that morning, but her hair seemed to
have eaten it. At least they had the same
lunchbox, even if Maisie Mae's was a bit,
well, *wormier* than Bethany's.

"I thought I was going to die!" said
Maisie Mae. "I opened it, and *thousands* of
worms tumbled out, onto the floor, into
my hair, *everywhere*!"

"Thousands?" gasped Bethany-next-
door in horror.

"Okay, there weren't exactly *thousands*. More like twenty. And they didn't fall out. But there *were* worms. I screamed the house down! And Mum came running, and she hugged me, and then she shouted at Harry and Ollie, who had to put the worms back in the garden, even though they wanted them for fishing, and then they were banned from ever fishing again in *their entire lives*.

And then they cried, and begged me for forgiveness. Then we washed the lunchbox out with extra-hot, extra-soapy water."

"Sounds horrible!" said Bethany-next-door, who always knew

just what to say in these situations.
"A complete worm-shock!"

"Worm-nightmare!" Maisie snorted.
"**WORM-TASTROPHE!**"
Bethany giggled.

"And then," continued Maisie Mae,
"Harry said that I should like worms,
because I like *anything* pink!"

"Ugh! Your brothers are *awful*," said
Bethany-next-door, rolling her eyes.
"Honestly, Maisie Mae, I don't know how
you kept calm."

Maisie Mae smiled. "I didn't. I threw
a worm at Harry, and Mum told me off
too!" They both burst out laughing.

Maisie Mae opened her lunchbox.
"Anyway, I got my lunchbox back. Harry
and Ollie won't get their hands on it
again." She took a bite of sandwich, and

screwed up her face in disgust. "Ughhh!" she moaned, spitting her mouthful out into her hand. "Marmite!" she said.

"Don't you like Marmite?" asked Bethany.

"No!" exclaimed Maisie Mae, peering into the sandwich. "Especially when it's got added *fish food*!" She pulled the sandwich open to show Bethany the tiny little coloured flakes that they used to feed the family goldfish.

Marmite +
fish food
= YUCK!

"I think I'm going to be sick," said Bethany-next-door faintly.

"I think *I'm* going to KILL my brothers!" said Maisie Mae. She stood up and looked around the dinner hall.

The twins were seated a few tables away. Ollie noticed her looking and nudged Harry. Harry waved a sandwich in the air and both boys burst out laughing.

Maisie marched over to them, her face hot with anger. "Give me back my peanut-butter sandwiches!" she demanded.

"What, you mean *these* peanut-butter sandwiches?" Harry asked, innocently.

Maisie lunged at Harry, but he quickly stuck out his tongue and licked his sandwich before she could snatch it back.

Maisie then turned to Ollie, who stuffed an entire sandwich into his mouth.

"Mum's *sooo* going to hear about this!" she said.

Ollie shrugged. "*Mmf mmm mum-mmm mmf!*"

Maisie Mae started to march off in a grump, but as she turned she noticed Harry's crisps on the table in front of him. Suddenly, she had a brilliant idea. She quickly turned back and bashed her fist down on the packet as hard as she could. Maisie grinned as it exploded, spraying Harry and Ollie with tiny fragments of cheese and onion crisps. Everyone around them laughed as Maisie Mae went back to sit next to Bethany-next-door.

"I HATE my brothers!" she said.

"They're the *worst*," said Bethany-next-door sympathetically. "Here, you can have some of my lunch." She pushed some neat sandwich triangles over to Maisie Mae.

And that was why Maisie Mae liked Bethany-next-door. Bethany knew *exactly* what a **TERRIBLE** problem brothers were, and she always shared her sandwiches. Maisie Mae knew they would be best friends for ever, until they were old and wrinkly and had to walk with sticks. They had already decided that they were **ALWAYS** going to live next-door to each other, even when they were grown up and lived in huge pink palaces.

Maisie Mae spent lots of time at Bethany's house, so she knew what an

absolute complete and utter **HEAVEN**
it was to have no brothers and sisters at
all. She thought Bethany-next-door was
SO lucky. She had a room all to herself,
and she could even leave her Sylvanian
Families out without them being used in
an Action Man aerial attack.

They shared Bethany's lunch (a
proper *girly* lunch, with posh ham triangle
sandwiches with the crusts
cut off, an iced
cupcake, and
a good-for-
you fruity yogurt –
definitely **NO** worms
and **NO** fish food),
and tried to take their
minds off all things
brother-shaped.

Posh sandwich +
cupcake + yoghurt
= YUM!

♥ 23 ♥

Maisie Mae was grateful, but couldn't help thinking that her peanut-butter sandwiches would have been tastier.

"Ohmygollygosh, I nearly forgot. **BIG NEWS!**" said Bethany-next-door. "Mum says I'm allowed to decorate my room!" Bethany's mum was *so* cool, and was *always* letting her do amazing things and get brilliant new stuff. "She said I'm allowed to choose the paint and a new duvet cover **AND** new curtains and lampshades and everything!" she continued.

Maisie Mae was amazed, and not at all jealous.

Well, maybe a teensy bit.

All right, she was **COMPLETELY** jealous, but happy for Bethany too. "But I love your yellow room just as it is," she told Bethany.

Bethany-next-door grinned so hard it looked like her face was going to break in two. "When I'm done with it, it's going to be *way* better."

"You don't mean—"

"I certainly do!"

"It's going to be …" Maisie gasped.

Bethany squealed. "And I want *you*, Maisie Mae, to help me choose."

"Choose what?" asked Maisie Mae.

"Everything, of course! The paint,

the lampshades, the duvet cover –
EVERYTHING! After all, what are
best-friends-that-are-almost-as-good-as-
sisters for?"

Maisie Mae couldn't believe it. She was
going to help turn Bethany's room into a
perfect pink paradise!

CHAPTER THREE

Family Meeting

Maisie Mae dashed home from school. She went to her room and slammed the door, pushing a chair behind it so the twins couldn't get in.

She soon heard banging on the other side.

"Let us in, runt!" shouted Harry.

"I'm getting changed!" she shouted back.

"Leave her alone, boys!" called Mum from downstairs. Maisie Mae waited until they had grumbled off down the stairs and quickly got changed. Then, checking the chair was still firmly in place, she fished under her bed for her box of girly stuff, hidden safely away from the boys.

"Aha!" she said as she found the **PERFECT** thing – a big pot of sparkly glitter. Maisie chuckled at the wicked plan of revenge in her head.

She pulled the bedroom door open quietly, and sneaked over to the bathroom. She looked around until she found the twins' extra-large pot of cool-boy hair gel. She knew that they never left the house without covering their heads with the icky-sticky stuff. She poured the glitter slowly into the gel, stirring it around with the end of a toothbrush to make sure it was well mixed in.

"This should get them back for my
worm-horror and sandwich-terror!" she
said happily to herself. She was just mixing
in the last bit when she heard Dad call
from downstairs.

"ATTENTION ALL SPROGS! FAMILY MEETING! KITCHEN! NOW!"

The house shook with the **THUMP-THUMP-THUMP** of boy-feet running to the kitchen. Maisie Mae screwed the lid back on the gel and rushed down the stairs too. They hardly ever had family meetings in their house, which meant that something **VERY BIG** must be happening.

Everyone gathered around the kitchen

table. Maisie Mae's twelve-year-old brother, Jack, was still in his football kit from school, his lanky legs covered in mud. *This* must *be important,* thought Maisie Mae, as Mum hadn't told him off for wearing his dirty boots in the house.

Josh, her eldest brother, sat at the end of the table, his mop of long hair covering his eyes.

"Josh, can you take your

earphones out, please?" Mum said with a mime, so he could work out what she was saying.

This is *serious,* thought Maisie Mae. *Super-super serious* – Josh hadn't taken his earphones out since Christmas. Maisie was pretty sure he wore them even when he was asleep. Harry even stopped punching Ollie in the arm so he could pay attention.

Maisie Mae was suddenly scared that Dad was about to tell them something **AWFUL**, like she was getting another brother. Another boy to make Maisie even more outnumbered. He'd probably take her room, and Maisie would have to sleep in the shed, with the ants and the spiders and …

"Settle down, boys!" Dad interrupted her thoughts. Maisie Mae coughed. "*And* Maisie. We've got a **BIG ANNOUNCEMENT!**"

"Not another baby?" Maisie said with a groan.

"No!" Mum laughed.

"You found that toaster we buried?" said Harry.

"No," Mum replied. "Hang on, what toaster?"

"The neighbours are complaining again, aren't they?" Josh interrupted.

"What? No! Stop guessing!" said Dad. "We've had a bit of sad news. My Uncle Sam, from America, passed away last week."

♥ **33** ♥

"What does 'passed away' mean?" said Ollie, who was trying to throw grapes from the fruit bowl into Harry's mouth. Most of them were splattered on the wall behind him.

"He kicked the bucket," Josh told him.

"Josh! Have some respect!" said Mum. "Sadly, Ollie, it means he died."

Maisie fiddled with the frazzled ends of her sleeves. She'd only met Dad's Uncle Sam once, but he'd been really cool. He'd worn a crazy colourful shirt and brought them all a present. Maisie's had been a super-special Disney Princess T-shirt, which you could only get from America. Bethany-next-door had **ADORED** it and had been *sooo* jealous. She and Maisie Mae had taken turns wearing it, until the twins had

used it as part of a
homemade parachute.

"He was very old
and he had a really good life,"
Dad continued. "And there's nice
news, too. He left us some
money in his will."

"**BRILLIANT!**"
shouted Harry and
Ollie at the same time.
The kitchen burst into
uproar: Josh started
drumming on the
table, Jack pulled his
shirt over his head like
he'd just scored a goal,
and the twins ran around
the table yelling, "We're
rich! We're rich!"

Maisie Mae just stood in the middle of the craziness and rolled her eyes at her brothers, but secretly she was already planning what she and Bethany-next-door could do when they both had their own ponies to ride.

"**QUIET!**" shouted Dad, and everyone settled down. "We're NOT rich—"

"We're moving to a mansion!" Jack interrupted.

"With a swimming pool!" yelled Harry.

"And a bowling alley!" Josh agreed.

"And a zoo!" Maisie couldn't help joining in.

"With monkeys!" added Ollie.

"I'm afraid we still can't afford to do any of those things," Mum interrupted. "Especially not the monkeys."

"We've got enough monkeys in this house already," Dad agreed. "But, **ANYWAY**, while we can't move, we *do* have enough money to make *this* house a bit bigger."

Maisie Mae looked at her brothers. They looked as confused as she felt.

"We're going to make the loft into a brand new bedroom," said Mum.

"**SHOTGUN!**" shouted Maisie Mae quickly. She and her brothers always yelled it when they wanted to claim the front seat of the car.

"Sorry, sweetie," said Mum. "That's only for the car."

"Yeah, doofus!" said Jack. "It's 'bagsy' you mean. **BAGSY THE NEW ROOM!** It's mine!"

"No, Jack, no 'bagsy'," said Dad. "And no 'dibs' either," he said, stopping Josh from shouting it. The whole kitchen seemed to moan at the same time, and everyone started to shout about how *they* deserved the room.

"I need a room to myself to practise my guitar," said Josh. "How can I become a rock god with Jack in my face the whole time?"

"I need room for all my sports stuff," said Jack, jumping up and down.

"I wouldn't have to leave my sweaty shin pads and muddy hockey boots in the hall all the time!"

"Hmm … that *would* be nice," agreed Mum.

"We get double dibs—" Harry started.

"—'cos we're twins!" Ollie finished.

"I just want a room that doesn't smell like a massive armpit!" said Maisie Mae. "Besides, I'm **THE ONLY GIRL**! I shouldn't have to share with **BOYS!**"

"That's a very good point, Maisie, and we'll bear that in mind," Mum said.

Maisie stuck her tongue out at

her brothers, who started shouting how **UNFAIR** that was.

"BUT," Mum continued, "you've *all* got good reasons not to have to share."

"**HA!**" Josh said to Maisie.

Maisie sat down with a bump.

"And, of course," said Dad, when the family had settled down, "your mother and I couldn't possibly choose between you all."

"Of course you can! Just pick your favourite!" said Josh, with a cheeky wink, pointing to himself.

"So," said Mum, ignoring him, "what we're going to do is think about it **VERY CAREFULLY** over the next few weeks. We'll be looking at everyone's behaviour so we can make our decision."

Everyone knew what that meant,

especially Maisie Mae – whoever was the best behaved would have the new room *all to themselves*.

The kitchen suddenly went super-silent, except for Arthur Stanley, who let out a loud **PARP** from his nappy.

Maisie grinned. She knew she could beat her brothers at bestest behaviour any day. She sat up straight, and put on her **SERIOUSLY DETERMINED** face.

SERIOUSLY DETERMINED FACE

She looked over at her messy collection of brothers, who sat around the table covered with mud and hair and bogies.

Easy peasy, she thought. In a few weeks, she was going to get a Perfectly Pink, Extra-Girly, **NO-BOY ZONE** of her very own!

CHAPTER FOUR

Sticky Stars and Dirty Tricks

Maisie Mae ran straight next door after the meeting and rang Bethany's doorbell in her special secret-code way – four rings one after another, then one extra-long *riiiiiiing*.

She was only halfway through the long *riiiiiiing* when Bethany's mum wrenched the door open, a slightly pained look on her face. "Hello, Maisie Mae," she said, tiredly. "Bethany and I were just up in her bedroom. Did you have a good day?"

"Yes, it was super-exciting," Maisie told her as she followed Bethany-next-door's mum upstairs. Bethany was sitting on her bedroom floor. All her puppy and kitten posters had been taken down, and there were splodges of different shades of pink on her yellow bedroom wall, rather like there had been an explosion in a candyfloss factory.

"What are you doing?" Maisie asked.

"We're choosing the paint for my room!" said Bethany-next-door, with an excited grin.

"Bethany says you're going to help her," said Bethany's mum. "But you'd better sit down first and tell us about your exciting day."

Maisie Mae told them all about the great news. "My dad had a **RICH UNCLE** who lived far away, probably in a **CASTLE** or something, and he died last week in *suspicious circumstances*. Dad got a letter saying he'd been left a **MYSTERIOUS FORTUNE**, but" – Maisie lowered her voice and stared at Bethany – "the money is **CURSED!**"

Bethany gasped, while her mum frowned at Maisie Mae in an 'Oh, really?' sort of way.

"All right, it's not cursed," Maisie continued, "but it *is* enough to put a whole new bedroom on top of our house! It's going to be the **BEST!**"

She explained that Mum and Dad had started a good-behaviour competition, and they'd be watching them all very carefully.

"I'm definitely going to beat the boys!" Maisie grinned. "After all, I'm the sweetest and loveliest by *far*."

Bethany's mum smiled. "You'll still have to be extra-specially well-behaved if you want that room to yourself."

She was right, and all of a sudden Maisie had a Horrid Thought – for all she knew, the boys could be out-behaving her *right now*.

"I've got to go!" she said as she jumped up. "I'm going to help Mum with dinner!"

Back next door, it was strangely quiet: Josh's music wasn't blaring out from upstairs, Harry and Ollie weren't rolling around on the floor or dive-bombing each other, and Jack wasn't in the front room shouting at a rugby match on the telly. Instead, the boys were all sitting silently around the kitchen table, backs straight, their hands placed neatly in their laps. In fact, if Arthur Stanley hadn't been blowing bubbles in his milk, Maisie Mae would have been worried that there'd been a secret invasion while she'd been next door, and that her brothers had all been turned into brain-eating zombies. She peered at them, looking for any signs of intelligent life – which was hard enough to find normally.

"Sit down, Maisie," Mum told her. "I've made a star chart so I can track how well everyone is doing," she said, showing them a brightly coloured sheet of paper stuck to the fridge door. "It's got all your names on it. Harry and Ollie, you said you'd like to share a room, even if you get the new one, so you just have one entry between you."

"Yes!" the twins said, high-fiving each other.

"But that doesn't mean you get twice the number of stars," said Mum.

"Oh." Ollie moaned. "But can we be called 'Team Twin'?"

"Or 'Double Trouble'?" Harry joined in.

"No," said Mum briskly. "We'll give you

a star if Dad and I think you have behaved well, or take one away if you've behaved badly. The person with the most stars by the time the room is ready will get it *all to themselves*."

That evening, Maisie Mae felt like she had walked into some weird TV show about perfect families. She helped Mum by laying the table, making sure every knife and fork was perfectly straight. She even got the best napkins out and tried to fold them into pretty shapes, like a swan or an angel, but they kept flopping around so she ended up settling for triangles. Jack was in the back garden, feeding their rabbit, Batman Flopsy, and for once Jack was dressed in normal clothes, not his usual sweaty sports kit.

Is this what living in a normal *family is like?* wondered Maisie.

"Good work, you two," said Mum as Jack came inside. "A star for each of you." She peeled off two super-shiny sticky stars and put them next to Jack and Maisie's names on the chart. Maisie smiled proudly.

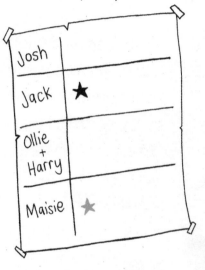

Josh	
Jack	★
Ollie + Harry	
Maisie	★

At dinner, the whole family ate in silence, with no shouting, screaming or bodily noises whatsoever (well, except for Arthur Stanley, whose burps and trumps seemed extra loud in the quiet room).

"Could you pass the tomato sauce please, Joshua?" said Jack politely.

Josh passed the bottle over with a smile, without giving a usual rude reply like, "Get it yourself, fart-face!"

"This makes a change," said Dad. "Isn't it nice to have a meal without any burping?"

"**BURP!**" went Arthur Stanley.

"Well, without *much* burping, anyway," added Dad. "And chewing with your mouths closed! Well done, everyone."

"Thank you, Daddy," said Maisie Mae, giving him her cutest smile, the one she normally saved for when she wanted extra pocket money.

"*Thank you, Daddy!*" the twins mocked in squeaky voices, but under their breath.

"You've got cabbage in your teeth, lame-brain!" whispered Jack, elbowing her in the side. Maisie quickly dropped the smile and picked out a large piece of green leaf from between her front teeth.

At the end of the meal, Mum and Dad stacked up the plates.

"We'll do it!" said Ollie, jumping up with Harry.

"No!" said Mum quickly. "It's nice of you to offer, boys, but I don't want my plates involved in another game of kitchen Frisbee, like the last time you cleared up."

They all sat patiently at the table while Mum and Dad were in the kitchen. Maisie Mae was sitting next to Jack. She noticed that his leg was jumping up and down under the table like a pogo stick. Jack **NEVER** sat still. He was always playing sport and running about, so being on his best behaviour and keeping still for hours meant that he had stored up *a lot* of energy. Maisie Mae could see that he was trying to stop himself, but it was no good. He was close to bursting.

JACK ATTACK!

First he tapped his foot …

Then he drummed his fingers on the table …

His body wriggled …

He bit his lip, but couldn't sit still a second longer …

"**JACK ATTACK!**" he suddenly yelled, exploding with energy. He leapt up and **THREW** himself on Harry and Ollie, who grunted under his weight. Jack writhed and wriggled as the twins tried to wrestle him off. His leg kicked out, knocking the table so that Maisie Mae's glass of orange juice went all over Arthur Stanley.

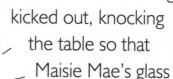

"**WAAAAAAAAAAH!**" cried Arthur Stanley. Maisie Mae picked up her glass to stop it rolling off the table.

"What on **EARTH** is going on?" said Mum as she came back into the room. Maisie Mae turned, and knew it looked bad. She was standing over Arthur Stanley with an empty glass, and the baby was even wetter and stickier than usual.

Maisie looked over at Jack, who was now sitting down, looking innocent.

"Maisie! I can't believe you did that!" he said, acting shocked.

Maisie looked at Mum, who shook her head and tutted.

"Me? **NO!**" shouted Maisie. "I didn't! I wouldn't! It was—"

"Maisie Mae, do I have to take your star off the chart already?" Mum asked.

Maisie looked from her mum to her smug brothers, took a deep breath and sat down. It was **SO UNFAIR**, but she definitely didn't want to lose her star. "Sorry, Mum," she mumbled. "Sorry, Arthur Stanley."

"That's better. Any more bad behaviour and you'll definitely lose a star, understand?"

Maisie Mae nodded sadly. As soon as Mum had left the room with Arthur Stanley to clean him up, she glared at Jack. "You'll pay for that!" she said, scowling her scowliest scowl.

"You should give up on the room now," said Jack. "It's going to be *mine*." He laughed and rubbed his hands together like an evil genius in a movie.

"Yeah, Monkey Mae!" said Josh. "You've got no chance."

Maisie Mae looked round at her brothers. "Just you wait," she said. "I'm going to get more stars than all of you put together! I'll get that room *all to myself*. You'll see." She stood up and slammed her fist down on the table. The boys exchanged worried glances. "This isn't a game any more. This is **WAR!**"

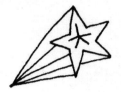

CHAPTER FIVE

REVENGE!

Maisie Mae got up early the next day without an alarm clock or her mum's extra-loud wake-up call from the landing. She jumped out of bed and was dressed in her school uniform before the twins had even opened their eyes and trumped underneath the covers. There was a reason for getting up so early —
REVENGE!

She was going to make Jack *pay* for getting her into trouble with Mum and almost making her lose a star. Maisie sneaked along the landing on tiptoes and listened outside the bathroom door. She could hear the sound of running water and the wailing sound of Jack singing in the shower:

"Man United! We're the best!
Man United! We'll beat the rest!
Tackle and score, we're number
      one!
If you want more, we'll kick your
      bum!"

"**JACK!** Keep it down, will you?" shouted Mum from downstairs. Jack stopped singing. Maisie Mae knew she didn't have much time.

Maisie went into Jack and Josh's room where Josh was still in his bed, snoring loudly like a hippo with a blocked nose. She knew what she had to do. Jack was always leaving his mucky football kit lying around, and it drove Mum *bonkers*. If she could hide some of it around the house, then Jack would lose a star for sure!

Maisie Mae giggled quietly at her fiendish plan and went about finding the kit. She carefully pulled out his long red and white football socks from his bag, holding her nose at the stench. Looking into the bag for more kit, Maisie

suddenly conjured up another cunning plan. If she replaced his shorts with …

She tiptoed quietly past Josh, who turned over with a grunt. "*Mmf* … Don't put the monkey in the fridge!" he muttered in his sleep. Maisie held her breath as she edged past him and out of the door. She rushed along to her room and came back with something in her hand. Hearing the shower switch off, she acted quickly, stuffing her secret weapon into Jack's kitbag. Then she **WHIZZED** out of the room and down the stairs just seconds before Jack emerged from the bathroom in a cloud of steam.

Downstairs, Maisie Mae nipped into the kitchen and shoved the pair of sweaty socks deep into Mum's pile of clean washing.

"When Mum finds these, you are going to be in **SOOOO** much trouble, Jack!" Maisie giggled to herself.

Smoothing down her skirt and patting her unruly hair back into place, she walked into the kitchen, trying hard to hold back a smile by putting on her ever-so-sweet-and-innocent face.

"Good morning, Maisie Mae!" said

Harry from the kitchen table. Maisie Mae glanced over at the twins and tried to work out what was wrong. Then she realised: Harry and Ollie looked perfect – their hair was washed and combed, their ties were straight and their uniforms were neat and tidy. They smiled at Maisie.

"You look creepy," she said. Her brothers were *never* this perfect. They were never quiet, never sat still, and certainly never called her by her actual name. They normally called her something like Bog-breath or Snot-face. "What are you up to?" she asked.

"Us?" said Ollie. "Nothing, just saying good morning. Would you like some breakfast?" He offered her the large packet of chocolatey chocolate balls.

Maisie snatched the box from him before he had time to pour it down the back of her shirt or something equally **HORRID**. She poured herself a bowl and tucked in. The boys smiled again and continued to eat their sugary honey-flakes.

"Good morning, gang!" said Mum as she rushed through the kitchen. She was carrying a stack of mugs, Arthur Stanley clinging to her leg like a baby chimp. "Harry, Ollie, did you clean out Batman Flopsy's hutch?"

"Yes, Mum!" sang the twins.

"Excellent!" she said. "Good work. At this rate you'll be getting a new star on the chart in no time." Mum limped out of the kitchen, trying to prise Arthur Stanley from her leg.

"I don't believe you did it," said Maisie Mae, as soon as Mum had gone.

Harry and Ollie gave a fake gasp of shock and turned to each other, pretending to cry.

"You're *up* to something!" said Maisie, waving an accusing spoon at them. She chewed, puzzled, on another mouthful of cereal, and that was when her brothers broke out in smiles – not small, sweet, angelic ones, but big, nasty, *evil* ones.

"That's where you're wrong, Maisie *Moo!*" said Harry. "We *did* clean out the rabbit hutch, first thing this morning. It was full of rabbit poop – little, brown, round poops …"

Maisie Mae stopped chewing.

"We weren't sure where to put them," said Ollie. "So we just put them in the nearest box we could find."

They both looked at Maisie's cereal.

"Whaaaaat?" cried Maisie Mae, her mouth full of half-chewed breakfast.

"That's what extra-chocolatey chocolate balls are made of, after all!" said Harry, rubbing his hands with glee. "Why do you think there's a cartoon rabbit on the box?"

Maisie took one look at her bowlful of brown milk and floating round pellets, and **SCREAMED!** She ran to the kitchen tap and turned it on full, sticking her mouth under the flowing water.

"What's going on?" said Mum, rushing

back into the kitchen.

"They made me eat rabbit poop cereal!" shouted Maisie Mae.

Mum's face turned into a glare and she looked over at Harry and Ollie, who were rocking with laughter.

"**BOYS!**" shouted Mum, silencing the twins. She went to over Maisie Mae and gathered her up in a big hug. "Hush now, Maisie Mae. They were just joking."

"Are you sure? There's definitely no poop? You promise?" wailed Maisie.

"I promise. There is absolutely, definitely, positively *no* rabbit poop in your cereal. And as for you, boys …" Mum went over to the fridge and peeled a star off Harry and Ollie's chart.

"No way!" said Ollie. "She just can't take a joke!"

"Aw, Mum!" said Harry.

Mum stood firm. She crumpled up the sticky star and threw it in the bin.

"That's what you get for teasing your sister!" she said. "You're lucky I don't take away two. Come on, Maisie Mae, you'll be late."

Maisie took her mum's hand and followed her out of the room, but couldn't resist turning back to the boys and sticking out a chocolate-brown tongue at them. *Hmmmmm,* she thought. *I think I'll get them to tease me more. They'll lose loads of stars! I might even cry next time …*

In the school playground, Maisie Mae told Bethany-next-door all about her breakfast blow-out with the twins.

"… and then I *screamed* and ran my mouth under the tap. I mean, of course, they didn't fool me for one teensy-tiny minute, but I wanted to make sure that Mum took a star away," Maisie boasted.

Bethany-next-door's mouth hung open in amazement. "Ugh! How utterly, utterly *horrid*! You could have been rabbit-pooped to **DEATH!**"

"I *know*!"

Bethany put a friendly arm around

Maisie Mae's shoulders. "Don't worry, Maisie. I'll help you get your own back!" she said. "Uh oh! Here come your **AWFUL** brothers now!"

Maisie saw Harry and Ollie walking across the playground. As they walked, everyone stopped what they were doing to point and laugh at them.

The twins looked at each other in confusion. Harry jumped back as he saw his brother's hair sparkling in the sunlight. "P-p-pink!" he stuttered. "Your hair's pink!"

"So's yours!" said Ollie. "Perfectly pink glitter gel! How did—?"

The boys faces' creased into frowns of fury as they finally realised how they had ended up looking like giant raspberry-ripple ice-cream cones.

"MAISIE MAE!" they yelled,
looking around for their sister.

"Don't worry, Bethany," smiled Maisie
Mae, already running off to hide. "I've
already had my revenge!"

CHAPTER SIX

Absolute GENIUS!

When she got home after school, Maisie Mae was determined to get another star. "I'll cook dinner!" she said with a smile, but Mum's face fell.

"Um ... that's okay, thanks. I've got it all under control!" she said. "Besides, I still haven't got the mess off the ceiling from the time you tried to make banana pasta." She lifted Arthur Stanley from his buggy and plopped him down on the

Banana pasta, anyone?!

floor. Maisie Mae saw her chance. "Okay, then, I'll babysit Arthur Stanley while you make the dinner," she said, grabbing her little brother and giving him a cuddle. "But I *don't* do nappies!"

"Thank you, Maisie! That would be really helpful," Mum said.

Maisie smiled and carried Arthur Stanley through to the lounge. She plonked him down in a heap of his toys and dashed back to the door, then sneakily peered through to the kitchen, where she saw Mum placing another star next to her name on the chart.

"Yes!" she whispered. "Gimme five, lil' bro!" She held up her hand, but Arthur Stanley simply dribbled and let out a loud trump.

Just then the front door burst open. **"MAISIE MAE!"** came a yell. **"WHERE ARE YOU?"**

"Uh oh," Maisie whispered to Arthur Stanley. "Jack's back!"

Jack came into the room, still caked in mud from football practice and looking … odd. Maisie looked him up and down, and tried to place what was different. Everything looked all right: football boots … shin pads … tutu …

Riiight, thought Maisie Mae. *I think I*

know why he might be angry with me ... my secret weapon!

"Maisie! I am going to **KILL** you until you are **DEAD!**" shouted Jack.

"Hi, Jack! How was football?" said Maisie with a smile, trying to pretend nothing was wrong.

"How was football? How to you **THINK** it was?" said Jack, his eyes wide with fury. His face had turned a dangerous shade of red, like an angry tomato. "Does anything give you a clue? **DOES IT?**"

♥ 77 ♥

Maisie Mae bit her lip to stop herself laughing. It didn't work, and she let out a great big "**HA!**"

"Nope," she said, through the tears of laughter. "You look very pretty, though!"

"*Aaargh! That's it!*"

Maisie Mae screamed as Jack chased her through the lounge and into the kitchen. She picked up Arthur Stanley on the way to use as a human shield, but he chose that moment to fill his nappy. His face went red with concentration

and his bottom exploded, filling the air with a toxic stench.

"Ugh!" said Maisie, holding him at arm's length.

"What on earth is going on?" said Mum. Mum stood in the doorway with the two workmen who had started building the new room in the loft. She took the stinky baby off Maisie. "Can't you keep it down? I'm just making a cup of tea for the workmen."

"Maisie put her tutu in my football kit!" Jack yelled. "It was the third time I had got the wrong kit, so Coach made me wear it anyway."

"Maisie, is this true?" asked Mum.

"Not exactly," said Maisie Mae. "I think Jack *wanted* to wear it!"

"Mum, can I kill her? Please?" said Jack.

Mum pushed the two of them out of the kitchen. "No! Now be quiet, both of you. Jack, get in the shower. Maisie, that star is coming right off the chart."

"**MUM!**" moaned Maisie Mae.

Jack grinned triumphantly.

Just then, Bethany-next-door appeared in the doorway, with her mum just behind her.

"Sorry, the door was open," said Bethany. "Nice tutu, Jack!"

"Yeah, pink is *so* your colour!" Maisie snorted.

Jack made a lunge for the girls, who squealed and dashed up the stairs, their feet thumping as they went. They clattered along the landing and burst into Maisie Mae's room, slamming the door behind them and wedging it closed with a chair. They collapsed on Maisie's bed in a fit of breathless giggles.

"Can you see how **TOTALLY** unfair that was?" said Maisie Mae.

"I *know*," said Bethany. "I thought Jack looked lovely!' Suddenly, her eye was caught by something. 'Um, Maisie? What's that?"

Maisie Mae looked at the pile of brown sludge in the middle of Harry's bed. Bethany-next-door looked a bit sick. Maisie Mae looked closer, and breathed a sigh of relief.

"It's okay," she said. "It's just a half-chewed Mars bar."

Maisie looked around at the messy room. There were toys, clothes, food and junk strewn *everywhere*, and all of it belonged to Harry and Ollie. "Aargh! Stupid, messy boys!" she said in frustration. "We can't play in here. This is why I need a bedroom of my own."

Bethany-next-door nodded wisely. "It must be rubbish not being able to play in your own room," she said.

Maisie Mae nodded.

They checked the coast was clear on the landing by pressing their ears up to the door. There was no sound of Jack, so they headed out onto the landing towards the stairs.

"Things will be better when I've got my **BRILLIANT** new room." Maisie sighed as she pointed up to where a hatch in the ceiling was open. They could see up to the rafters in the roof. The workmen had left it open while they had their tea break, and there was dust and dirt everywhere.

"They're making an awful mess!" Bethany said. "Can we go up and look?"

Maisie sighed again. "No. Dad is being mega-boring and says it's dangerous. We're not allowed up there on pain of death, or **WORSE!**" She looked down at the mess on the carpet and kicked it around a bit with her shoe. A thought suddenly formed in her mind. "Oh!" she said. "I. Am. Brilliant! I don't know how I get these *fantastic* ideas! I must be a **GENIUS!**"

"Uh oh," said Bethany-next-door. "If you're having a *fantastic* idea, then someone's going to get into trouble!"

"It's *so* simple!" Maisie continued. "If

Dad and Mum think that one of the boys has been up in the loft, then they'll get into trouble and lose a star!"

"Hmm," said Bethany. "I think the idea was for you to try and get *more* stars than your brothers, not to make them *lose* theirs."

"**PAH!**" said Maisie. "It's *practically* the same thing, if you think about it!"

Bethany wasn't so sure. "How will you get one of your brothers to go up in the loft? I mean, they're not *that* stupid."

Both the girls burst out laughing then – they knew that Maisie's brothers were *exactly* that stupid. But Maisie Mae had other plans. She had spotted Josh's huge trainers lying on the landing, and now she picked one up. She slipped it on her foot and then stamped on the clean carpet. It left a great, big, dirty footprint.

"Mum and Dad will just *think* that Josh has been up there." She grinned. "What did I tell you? **GENIUS!**"

Maisie threw a trainer to Bethany, who caught it and held her nose.

"Ugh! **BOY-FEET!**"

Maisie rubbed the trainer she was holding around in the building dust and grinned when Bethany did the same. "Now for phase two of the plan!" she said. "Follow me!"

Maisie put on the right shoe and Bethany the left. "We need to make BIG steps!" Maisie commanded. "Think **BOY!**"

"Yuck!" Bethany stuck out her tongue. "Do I *have* to?"

The girls made great big steps along the landing, staggering and giggling, like they were in a mad three-legged race with huge clown-feet. They nearly fell over twice, finally stumbling into Jack and Josh's room and onto Josh's bed, crashing down on his duvet in a fit of laughter.

"I have to admit, Maisie Mae, that was a genius plan!" said Bethany. "Who knew that getting boys in trouble could be so much fun?"

Once they had stopped giggling, the girls carefully put Josh's trainers back, then went downstairs to get a glass of juice each. They passed the lounge which, after school, became the **BOY-CAVE**. All Maisie Mae's brothers were in there, doing *boy* things, being *boys*, and generally behaving *boyishly*. Maisie poked her head around the door and saw Josh and Jack on the sofa, staring like zombies at a football video game on the TV. Arthur Stanley sat at their feet, and Harry and Ollie were hidden behind the sofa. They were reaching into Mum's handbag, and handing Arthur Stanley things from it.

"Um …" said Bethany-next-door. "Should Arthur Stanley be wearing lipstick?"

Maisie Mae looked more closely at her baby brother.

The toddler was happily drawing all over his face with Mum's favourite red lipstick – the super-posh one Dad had got her for her birthday – while the twins giggled behind the sofa, and the older brothers sat playing their game. Arthur Stanley had red make-up on his mouth, teeth, cheeks and forehead, making him look like a surprised clown.

"I guess Josh is meant to be looking after him, and Harry and Ollie are trying to make him lose a star!" explained Maisie Mae. "See, Bethany? It's like a *war zone* in this house. If I want that new room, I've got to **FIGHT** for it!"

They carried on to the kitchen, Bethany-next-door shaking her head in amazement. "I've said it before, and I'll say it again, Maisie," she said. "Having so many brothers makes life completely, *utterly* and absolutely **CRAZY!**"

CRAZY!

CHAPTER SEVEN

Band Practice

"For the last time, Mum, I don't know what you're talking about!" said Josh.

It was Saturday morning and everyone was sat around the kitchen table, eating breakfast.

Mum was holding up a dusty pair of trainers and frowning. "Oh, well," she said. "I

wanted to give you a chance to own up. I didn't want to have to do this." She went to the fridge and peeled a star off Josh's chart.

"*Mum!*" protested Josh. "It wasn't me!"

Maisie Mae sat at the table, trying hard not to give herself away by laughing. She crammed her mouth full of extra-chocolatey chocolate balls so she wouldn't be able to speak, but she could feel her shoulders rocking up and down.

Luckily, Josh didn't notice. "It must have been Jack!" he shouted. "Stay out of my stuff, zit-face!"

Jack started to yell back, but Mum interrupted in her *I've-had-enough* voice. "I don't want to have to say this again," she bellowed. "Stay out of the loft! It's dangerous up there."

Josh	★★☆
Jack	★★☆★☆
Ollie + Harry	-☆
Maisie	★★

"Yeah, *Josh*!" said Maisie. She had finally finished her mouthful. She grinned at her brother, who shot an angry look back.

"It's not nice to gloat, Maisie Mae," said Mum. "And, anyway, I'm disappointed in all of you. Just look at the state of the star chart!"

The chart was stuck to the fridge, but there were hardly any stars stuck on it. Josh was down to three stars, while Jack had five. Maisie Mae saw to her **HORROR** that she only had two, and the twins were down to *minus* one!

"I demand a recount!" said Ollie.

Maisie was fairly sure he didn't know what that meant, but thought it sounded good. "I'm sure mine is wrong, too," she said. "I've been an *angel!*"

"You should *all* have more stars by now," said Mum. "If you want the new room, then you're all going to have to work harder."

"But, like, how?" sighed Jack, playing table football with bits of cereal.

"Here's a thought, you could start with tidying your rooms. You could all earn a star that way," Mum suggested.

Maisie Mae saw her smile and realised that she was really enjoying making them all behave.

"Ugh!" said the boys at the mention of tidying their rooms. "Do we have to?"

Maisie saw her chance. *If the boys don't tidy their rooms,* she thought, *and I tidy mine, I'll definitely be a star ahead!* **MEGA!**

After breakfast, Maisie Mae went to her room, ready to be the best tidier **EVER**. She opened the door and sighed. *This is going to take ages,* she thought.

The twins were sitting on their bunk bed, reading comics and practising their burping.

Maisie started to make her bed, and Harry looked up. "Ugh, you're not really *doing* it, are you?" he said, with a frown of disgust.

"Of course! When I've got my **VERY OWN ROOM** I can be as messy as I like!" said Maisie, sticking her tongue out

at the twins. She busied
herself with tidying, which
mainly involved kicking her
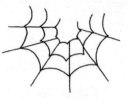
stuff under the bed and tucking the duvet
in until it all looked neat and clean (sort
of). The twins just looked on in silence.
As she finished, she turned to the boys
and grinned. "*I'm* going to get a star!" she
said, and turned to go
downstairs.

She had only got
as far as the stairs
when she heard
a *horrible*
noise
coming
from
Jack
and

Josh's room. She covered her ears. Maybe Jack was killing Josh! Or Josh was killing Jack? *Actually, it wouldn't be so bad if they did kill each other,* Maisie decided as she rushed towards the bedroom door. *It would be one less person to fight for the new room.*

She opened the door to Josh and Jack's room, expecting to see her brothers fighting, but instead found Josh

on his bed playing his guitar, while Jack
was **SINGING!** At least, Maisie Mae
thought he was singing – he was making a
high-pitched shriek with his throat, and it
sort of went in time with the guitar, so she
could only guess that that was what he
was doing.

"You sound like Beyoncé!" she said.

Josh stopped playing and burst out
laughing.

"Er, thanks, Maisie! I guess," Jack
replied.

"My friend Clare's cat, Beyoncé,"
continued   Maisie. "She
makes that   exact
same noise
when she's
having her fur
detangled!"

Jack just shook his head. "Some people just really don't appreciate art," he said, with a sniff.

"Yeah, go away, Maisie Mae!" Josh sneered. "You'll be sorry when we're a real band. We'll be so famous they'll make a movie about us!"

"Ha!" laughed Maisie. "Yeah, a horror movie!"

Josh got up to shoo Maisie Mae out of the room. "You'll see! We'll be mega-famous, and we'll even meet the **REAL** Beyoncé!"

Maisie was pushed out onto the landing and Josh slammed the door in her face. She was about to shout another insult at the closed door when—

"**MAISIE MAE!**"

It was Mum, and she was using her 'cross' voice (it was the same as her normal voice, but *a lot* louder). Maisie rushed to her bedroom.

"What sort of tidying do you call this?" Mum asked. Maisie pushed past her into the room. She looked around. The twin's side of the room was sparklingly spotless. The beds were made, the carpet clean and tidy, and all their clothes were hung up in the wardrobe. Maisie Mae was amazed, and confused, until she looked round and saw that *her* side of the room was a complete and total **TIP!** Toys, school work, clothes and books had been **FLUNG** everywhere! Harry and Ollie had struck again!

"Aaargh!" said Maisie. "**BOYS!** Stupid, stinky, grubby, brainless **BOYS!**"

CHAPTER EIGHT

Perfectly PINK Palace

Bethany-next-door's room was pink. *Actually*, thought Maisie Mae, *it's pinker than pink. It's* **PINK!** *with big capital letters and a fat exclamation mark at the end!* It was so pink that you could put a bright pink pony with pretty pink pigtails in there and it would be so camouflaged that you wouldn't be able to see it. *That would be a bit weird though*, thought Maisie, *and it would probably poop on the floor.*

"Bethany, it's … it's … perfect!" said Maisie Mae. "I'm sooooo jealous!"

"Thanks, best friend!" Bethany gave a happy twirl on her fluffy pink rug. "It's beautiful, isn't it?"

They sat down on Bethany's new pink unicorn duvet, each with a glass of pink strawberry smoothie, and Maisie told Bethany all about the twins' bedroom-untidying fiasco.

"Oh no!" said Bethany. "Did you lose a star?"

"Worse," said Maisie Mae. "I lost two! One for a messier-than-messy room, and one for shouting at Harry and Ollie and trying to flush their Xbox controllers down the loo. It's **SO** unfair!"

"How long is there left until the end of the competition?" asked Bethany.

"Only a week. Jack's already got nine stars and I'm on a big fat zero! So even if I'm extra-specially *amazingly* good every single day, there's no way I can catch up. It's been a complete

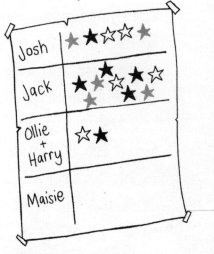

DISASTER!" Maisie sighed and blew bubbles in her pink smoothie. The worst thing was that Harry and Ollie got to go to the skate park all day, while *she* had to go back home and tidy her bedroom **AGAIN!**

Bethany put a friendly arm around her. "Don't worry, there must be something we can do," she said. "It sounds like what we need is some revenge planning, but something that's so surprising it'll stop them once and for all. Let's see … We could kidnap their Action Men?"

Maisie shook her head. "We'd have to find them first. And we'd never find them in that bedroom."

"Oh. What if we put lettuce in their sandwiches? They'd hate that!"

Maisie shook her head, glumly.

"Put salt on their cereal instead of sugar?"

"They do that anyway. They're a bit weird." Maisie sighed again. Bethany-next-door was a brilliant best friend, but when it came to brother-beating, her ideas were a bit rubbish.

"I'm sorry, Maisie." Now Bethany sighed. "I'm sure you'll get that room somehow, and I'll come and help you paint it pink, just like mine!"

Maisie felt a stirring in her brain as Bethany's words sank in. She looked through Bethany's bedroom door to the

landing, where there were lots of half-empty pots of pink paint and some brushes.

"Oh, *wow*!" said Maisie Mae. "I think I've got an idea!"

"Uh oh," said Bethany quietly.

"If I can't have my own perfectly pink palace in the new room, then I can just make my *old* room perfectly pink!"

"Ooh! I could help!" said Bethany, getting excited.

"Harry and Ollie will be out all day on their skateboards. We'll have plenty of time to redecorate while they're out! Come on, Bethany, let's go!"

The girls grabbed the pots of paint and paintbrushes and hid them in

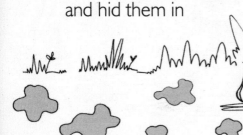

Bethany's giant Barbie Campervan, so they could wheel it round to Maisie's house. It was so heavy that the girls huffed and puffed as they pulled it, while the wheels creaked and complained.

"Wait, stop!" said Bethany, as they panted up the driveway. "There's Jack!"

Maisie stopped. Jack was over by the garage, throwing Harry and Ollie's school bags onto the roof. He was too busy swinging the boys' backpacks to notice them.

"Keep going!" said Maisie, and they waddled over to the front door and up the stairs, grunting with the effort. They burst into Maisie's bedroom and dropped the campervan onto the bed, the paint sloshing inside the tins.

"*Squee!*" squealed Maisie Mae. "I cannot believe it! My very own perfectly pink palace, at last! Let's get started!"

They pulled the pots of paint from their hiding place and tried to get the lids off, but they were tightly wedged.

"Mum used a screwdriver," said Bethany-next-door. She looked around and found an old Action Man leg under Ollie's bed, and handed it to Maisie Mae. "Here, try this!" After a bit of straining, the lid finally **POPPED** off, surprising Maisie so much that she dropped the the Action

Man leg into the paint. It sank to the bottom, and a glug of paint spilled onto the carpet.

Bethany gasped in horror, but Maisie just shrugged. "We'll clean that up later," she said confidently.

Maisie Mae dipped her paintbrush into the gooey, drippy paint and smiled. It was like having a giant pot of melted marshmallow! She dabbed a bit on the wall and spread it around carefully with the brush, like she'd seen her dad do when he decorated.

Bethany grabbed a

brush too, but after ten minutes they had
only covered a small bit of the wall.

Maisie Mae was getting bored.

"Let's speed this up a bit!" she said.
She scooped out a large amount of paint
with her brush, and **FLUNG** it at the
wall, pink paint splashing everywhere.

It didn't just hit the wall, however.

It hit the bed, the duvet cover, the carpet and even splashed onto Maisie's face and clothes. "Wow. It looks *awesome*!" she said with a laugh.

Bethany climbed up onto the bunk bed to get to the higher bit of wall. Paint streaked down the wall and dripped down onto the bed. The girls worked

hard, sloshing on the paint and rubbing it in with the brushes. When Maisie Mae needed to get the wall above her bed, she came up with the **BRILLIANT** method of jumping up and down on her mattress to get higher. Pink paint sprayed around her as she bounced, like a water sprinkler in summer.

"Um … Maisie …" said Bethany, pointing at the duvet. The faded Postman Pat was now covered in little pink spots.

"Oh, that'll come out in the wash!" said Maisie, trying to jump higher. She grinned as she completed a super-special-extra-high bounce, making a giant pink splodge on the ceiling. *It looks* **SO** *beautiful!* thought Maisie Mae. *This really was the best idea in the history of ideas* **EVER!**

CHAPTER NINE

Splodges and Speckles

A few hours later, when Maisie Mae and Bethany-next-door finally stood back to look at their work, Maisie suddenly wasn't so sure about her perfectly pink plan.

"It's, um …" said Bethany, frowning. "It's not *quite* the same as my room, is it?"

Maisie Mae shook her head in panic. There was pink paint on the wall. There was pink paint on the ceiling. There was pink paint on the bed, carpet, wardrobe, the chest of drawers and on their clothes, hair and skin. The two girls looked like they had caught a case of chicken pox; they were covered head to toe in paint splodges! The thing that Maisie couldn't understand was that it didn't even look very nice: the splodges on the carpet had dried into large, hard clumps, and the wall was patchy, the old wallpaper showing through in parts where the girls hadn't been able to reach with the brushes – even when they had stood on the bunk bed, Bethany hadn't been able to get to the edges of the wall, and then they had run out of paint.

"Oh … my … *goodness*! It's an absolute **DISASTER!** How did it go so wrong?" said Maisie Mae eventually. She looked around her room and felt a lump rise in her throat. Her voice started to wobble. "Do you think Mum and Dad will be cross?"

"It's not all bad," said Bethany, trying to cheer her friend up. "I like the spotty bits over there."

Maisie looked but couldn't see what she was talking about. "Um, I think that's

specks of paint on your glasses, Bethany," she said, gulping. She looked down. "And on my favourite jeans! These were my bestest going-out pair!"

Just then Harry and Ollie came barging through the door. They stopped in the middle of their conversation and stared in amazement at their newly decorated room.

At first they looked confused, as if they'd burst into the wrong house, but then they saw the girls in their splattered clothes. The twins looked at each other, grinned and let out a loud yell. "**MUM!**" they cried, and then both broke out into evil laughs.

"Wow, Maisie Mae!" said Harry, giving a slow hand-clap. "You've *really* done it this time!"

"Mum and Dad are going to be **SO** cross!" said Ollie, joining his brother in the mock-applause.

Maisie's tummy wobbled and she began to feel shaky just thinking about what her mum and dad were going to say. If she could turn back time, she'd go back and stop herself even picking up a paintbrush. Maybe if she wished *really* hard, it'd all go away. She squeezed her eyes shut.

"Don't be pink, don't be pink, don't be pink!" she muttered. She opened her eyes again, and her tummy did another bellyflop. The paint was still there. **ALL** of it!

Maisie heard Mum's footsteps coming up the stairs and felt her knees go weak. Beside her, poor Bethany-next-door hugged herself and started to cry, her breathing shaking with every sob. Slowly, Maisie came to realise a few things:

1) When Mum came through that door, she was in **BIG** trouble

2) Her perfectly pink palace was *far* from perfect

3) She would *definitely* lose a star for this

and …

4) Her old room was completely, stupidly, utterly and pinkly **RUINED!**

Maisie Mae stood in front of the paint-spattered wall. Bethany-next-door was making soft, sniffly noises. The twins were laughing so much that tears were streaming down their faces.

Maisie felt like crying too, but in a very different way. Mum and Dad were standing in front of her, their arms crossed, and their faces looking very, very cross **INDEED**.

"Harry, Ollie, downstairs." Mum snapped. "**NOW**."

The twins ran downstairs. As they went Maisie could hear them shouting to the others: "Josh! Jack! You'll **NEVER** guess what Maisie's done …!"

Dad rubbed his forehead in a *What-did-I-do-to-deserve-this-family?* kind of way.

"Maisie Mae, your father and I are very cross! Why did you think this was a good idea?" said Mum, rubbing Bethany-next-door's glasses frantically with a piece of cloth. "And dragging Bethany into it! What on earth possessed you? How am I going to explain this to her mum?"

Maisie knew that these were the type

of questions that weren't meant to be answered. If she did try to explain, she'd get into more trouble for being cheeky – she'd seen Jack do it loads of times. Instead, she looked down at the ground and tried to say sorry, but found that she couldn't even speak. She felt so guilty that the sobs were building up and not letting the words get through.

"It will come as no surprise to you that there will be no more stars for you," said Dad. "After *this* stunt, Maisie Mae, you will **DEFINITELY NOT** be getting the new room."

Josh	★ ★ ☆ ☆
Jack	★ ★ ★ ☆ ★ ★ ☆ ★ ★ ★ ★
Ollie + Harry	☆ ★
~~Maisie~~	

Maisie nodded, a tear dropping onto the paint-speckled floor.

While Mum took Bethany back next door to explain about the pink polka-dots on her clothes, face and hair, Maisie curled up on her bed and buried her face in her pillow miserably. She lay there for ages, only moving to slam the door when Josh and Jack came up to laugh at her. After a while there was a little tap on the door, and Mum's voice called, "Maisie? Can I come in?" Maisie opened the door and Mum came in and sat on the bed with her. "Do you have anything you want to say to me?" Mum asked.

Maisie Mae lifted her head to look at her mum. She was going to say how it was all so **UNFAIR**, and that she shouldn't have to share with **BOYS**

anyway, and that the room was better
pink, but all that came out was a sniffle.
"I'm so sorry, Mum," she said, throwing
her arms around her and giving a sob.
Mum hugged her and kissed her on
the head. "It's all right, sweetheart,"
she said.

They stayed there for a while and Maisie began to feel better. "Maybe Harry and Ollie will learn to like it?" said Maisie Mae, looking up with a cheeky grin.

Mum laughed. "Probably not."

Just then Maisie let out a moan and fell back into the hug with her mum.

"What's the matter now?" said Mum.

"I just realised," said Maisie Mae. "If I'm not getting the new room, that means I'm stuck in here with the twins **FOR EVER!**"

CHAPTER TEN

The Results

Over the next few days, Maisie Mae could only stand back and watch as her brothers battled against each other in the competition for the new room. She didn't join in the pranks and the sabotage, and she tried her hardest to be good, knowing that she had a lot of making up to do to Mum and Dad. She found that it was quite fun helping her mum in the kitchen, or joining Dad in the garden, and her brothers were too busy fighting with each other to play any mean tricks on her.

Josh pulled the old *Oh-look-Jack's-wet-the-bed* routine with a hidden water pistol, while Harry and Ollie planted an old chicken drumstick under Josh's bed for a few days in an attempt to stink out their room. Jack hit back by framing the twins – he scattered the DVDs from Dad's favourite boxset at the bottom of the garden and pretended that they had been practising clay-pigeon shooting with their Nerf guns.

By the end of the competition, the twins were down to minus six stars, while the rest of the chart looked pathetic. Between all the brothers, there were fewer stars than in a series of *I'm A Celebrity, Get Me Out of Here!*

On the final day, Mum and Dad called them all to the landing – where the staircase up to the new room had a ribbon tied across the front – to announce the winner. Mum stood proudly at the bottom of the steps, holding a pair of scissors like a celebrity at the opening of a new supermarket.

"We wanted to talk to all of you about the new room," said Dad. "Now, we *were* going to announce that Jack was the runaway winner of the star-chart challenge, with fourteen stars."

Jack jumped up and pumped the air with his fist. **"YES!** Aw, thanks! I'm so honoured!"

"Until," continued Dad, "we caught him sneakily awarding himself extra stars when no one was looking."

Maisie gasped. **"CHEAT!"**

Jack's smile faded, and then he just

shrugged. "Ah, well. Victory was nice while it lasted."

"No one has been particularly well behaved," said Mum with a tired sigh. "It would have been nice to have a normal, fair competition, but you were all more interested in getting each other to lose stars, rather than gaining them yourselves!"

Maisie Mae felt bad. She looked round at the boys and they looked a bit embarrassed, too: Josh scooped the hair out of his eyes to reveal a red face, and Harry and Ollie scuffed their feet on the floor, while Jack bit his fingernails, looking guilty. The only one who didn't look ashamed of himself was Arthur Stanley, who gurgled happily at Mum's feet.

"However, it *has* shown us how much you all want a room of your own," said Dad. He and Mum exchanged a look and smirked. "So, we are proud to declare this new loft conversion … **OPEN!**"

Mum snipped the ribbon and led the whole family up the new wooden staircase to the loft. One by one they climbed the steps, Mum and Dad going first with Arthur Stanley, followed by Josh, Jack, the twins and Maisie Mae. Being at the back, Maisie heard each of the boys' reactions as they got to the top of the steps.

"Woah!" said Josh.
"Wow!" said Jack.
"Cool!" said Harry.
"Yeah!" said Ollie.

"*Gumblebumblepoopitypoop!*" said Arthur Stanley.

"What?" said Maisie, eager to get up the steps and see the new room. "What's up there?" From the gasps of amazement she could only guess that the new room was so huge that it could fit a whole football pitch in there.

She got to the top of the steps and looked to her left. There was a brand new room, freshly painted and carpeted, with a cool skylight and a sloping ceiling where the roof was. But if she looked to her right, she saw **ANOTHER** brand new room, exactly the same.

"When the builders first put the floor down," explained Dad, "we realised how big the space was. So big, in fact, that we decided to put a wall up here and make two smaller rooms instead!"

Everyone ran around the empty rooms, jumping up to look out of the skylights. Maisie stood in the middle, feeling left out. She didn't know who would get

the new rooms; she just knew that it definitely wouldn't be her.

"This is awesome!" cried Ollie.

"Calm down, you lot!" said Mum. "If you want to know who gets to live here, then line up in a row!" The boys scattered into position like soldiers on parade. "You too, Maisie Mae!" Maisie drifted onto the end of the line.

"So we had to make a decision on who gets the rooms. We based our choice on who needed their own space the most, and who would use the rooms the best."

"I think Mum thinks she's a judge on *X-Factor*!" whispered Harry.

Josh and Jack snorted with laughter, but went silent again as Mum gave them a **LOOK**.

"The lucky person getting new room number one is …" said Dad, teasing them by taking his time. "Is …"

"Get-on-with-it!" blurted out Jack.

"Josh!" announced Mum.

Josh punched the air and gave a whoop of success. "Yes!" he said, pogoing around the new room and almost hitting his head on the sloping ceiling.

The others all looked disappointed,

until they realised that there was still room number two.

Mum continued. "The other new room is going to …"

Maisie Mae closed her eyes, held her breath and crossed her fingers and toes.

" … Harry and Ollie! Well done!" said Dad, laughing as the two boys started cheering and jumping up and down as well. The twins ran around their new room with their arms outstretched like aeroplanes.

Maisie Mae and Jack exchanged glum looks. "Arthur Stanley will move out of our room and in with you, Jack. You'll hardly notice he's there!"

Arthur Stanley let out an excited eardrum-bursting squeal, and Jack looked at Mum in a way that said **SERIOUSLY?**

Maisie Mae started to do some sums in her head. If Jack was having Arthur Stanley, and Josh and the twins each had a room of their own, that meant …

"I've got my own room, too!" shouted Maisie Mae, realising finally. "I'll be on my own! No boys! No worms! No **SMELL!** *Whoo-hooooooo!*"

Mum and Dad laughed as Maisie performed her own little celebration dance, her curly brown hair bobbing up and down, her arms punching the air above her.

"Well, you are the only girl, after all," said Mum.

"I said that *ages ago!*" said Maisie. "We could have saved a lot of bother if …" Maisie Mae looked at the expression on Dad's face and thought that this wasn't the best moment to argue. "I mean … **THANK YOU!**"

"Yeah, thanks, guys!" said Harry.

"You're the best!" said Ollie.

"There's even a bit of money left over for us to redecorate your rooms," said Dad. "Although *we'll* do the painting this time, if you don't mind, Maisie Mae!"

"Well, this is great," Jack said sulkily. "I'm the only one who isn't getting a room to himself, *and* I have to share with a smelly toddler!"

"Hey!" said Josh, wandering around his new room. "This place is much bigger than our old room, and it has got really good acoustics. If Jack moves up here with me, we could practise our music all the time! Whadya say, bruv?"

Jack looked in amazement at his brother, as did Mum and Dad. "Really? I wouldn't have to share with Stinky

Stanley? **MEGA!**" he cried, and high-
fived Josh.

"Cool," said Josh. "So we'll put a drum
kit here …"

Mum and Dad's smiles dropped as
Josh and Jack started making plans for
their band.

Everyone was happy, especially Maisie
Mae! At long last, she had her very own
room. She was going to make sure it was
absolutely, completely **PERFECT** in
every way.

CHAPTER ELEVEN

The Grand Tour

A few weeks later, the doorbell rang and Maisie Mae charged down the hall to the front door.

"I'll get it, I'll get it, I'll get it!" she chanted as she ran. She opened the door and found Bethany-next-door there with her mum.

"Come for the grand tour?" Maisie's mum asked. Arthur Stanley was perched on her hip, cheerfully blowing spit bubbles.

"Yes, please!" said Bethany-next-door's mum. "Maisie's told us all about her new room. Is it true that she has a painting on her wall of a dolphin sliding down a rainbow?

"Erm … I was *going* to, but we ran out of paint," said Maisie Mae. "Let's do the boys' rooms first, anyway! I want to save the best for last!" she continued, running up the stairs ahead of them.

At the very top of the second staircase, Maisie burst through the door to Josh and Jack's room, out of breath. "Mum … *puff* … calls this … *puff* … the penthouse."

They all shuffled into the first room, which held two beds. It was easy to tell which bed belonged to who – one side of the room was covered in posters for

bands and rock singers, and had a sign
above the bed which read: JOSH ROCKS!
The other side was plastered in football
posters, and had its own laundry basket
full of muddy sports kit. Jack also had a
signed Manchester United poster
above his bed. The wall in
between the posters had been
painted jet black, and in the
middle of the room sat
everything for their

band: a guitar,
a tambourine, a
whistle and two
bongo drums.

The boys hadn't managed to persuade
Mum and Dad to get a drum kit yet,
so they made do with a few cardboard
boxes and the set of bongos.

"Wow," said Bethany's mum. "It's
very … um … I mean, it's
so …"

"Smelly?" said Maisie.
"Somehow Josh and Jack
have managed to keep
the same pong as their old
room."

They moved over to the
twin's new room, and a look
of horror came over Mum's

face. The room was blue, with the same bunk bed in there, but it was *already* a complete mess! There were clothes on the floor, dirt on the carpet, and even a pair of pants hanging from the lightshade.

Harry and Ollie were both lying on the top bunk reading comics.

"**BOYS!** This room is an absolute tip!" said Mum.

"Calm down, Mum!" said Harry.

"Yeah, chillax!" said Ollie. "You said we could have our room exactly how we wanted it. And this is *exactly* how we want it!"

Mum shook her head and led them out,

muttering to Bethany's mum about messy little boys.

Maisie Mae stood at the top of the stairs, jumping with excitement. "Can we do *mine* now? I can't wait a single **SECOND** longer!"

"Go on, then!" said Mum with a smile.

Maisie squealed with delight as she dragged Bethany down the stairs to her new room. She paused outside the door, and put her hands over her friend's eyes.

"Maisie!" said Bethany. "I've been in your room loads of times before!"

"But this is my brand-spanking-amazingly *new*

room, and you're the FIRST to see it.
It's *completely* different. Don't peek!"
she said, opening the door and guiding
Bethany through. "Open your eyes …
NOW!"

Bethany-next-door looked around and
GASPED! "Wow, Maisie Mae! This is
PARADISE!"

The room had been completely
transformed. With the twins' bunk bed
gone, it looked huge, and Maisie had
painted the walls properly with Dad's
help. It wasn't the bright-shocking-pink
that she had wanted at first, but a pretty,
gentle, pastel shade. Mum had also
helped Maisie to paint some beautiful pink
flowers on the wall with a stencil set. She
had a **NEW** pink flower duvet – the
Postman Pat one hadn't survived the paint

splatters – and over the bed hung a pretty princess's canopy.

"It's beautiful," Bethany squealed. "A completely perfect **GIRLY** *girl's* room. Just what you wanted!"

There was a racket in the hallway and all the boys piled in at the doorway to see the new room. Harry and Ollie were the first through.

"Ugh!" cried Harry, making retching noises.

"Someone get a bucket!" said Ollie. Jack and Josh entered, too.

"Maisie, this is *soooo* uncool!" said Josh.

"Yeah," said Jack. "Pink is just so … so … what's the word?"

"**GIRLY!**" spat the twins.

Maisie Mae smiled and crossed her arms. "That's the *point*!" she said. "And I don't remember inviting you into **MY** room! Anyway, it's not quite finished. There is just one more thing …"

She shooed the boys out of the room and then reached under the bed. She picked up a sign that she'd carefully written in ultra-bright pink felt-tip:

KEEP OUT!
NO BOYS ALLOWED!

Maisie Mae hung it on the door and smiled wickedly at her brothers. "See you later, *boys*," she said, and swung the door firmly shut in their faces

Join Maisie Mae's

NO BOYS ALLOWED CLUB

**Sign up at www.lbkids.co.uk/noboysallowed
for free books, competition prizes,
news and more!**

READ MORE FROM MAISIE MAE!